A Father's Greatest Gift

OTHER BOOKS AND AUDIO BOOKS
BY KATHRYN JENKINS:

*To Your Health: Gospel Perspectives
on Nurturing the Mind, Body, and Spirit*

A Father's Greatest Gift

Kathryn Jenkins

Covenant Communications, Inc.

Cover image *O' Christmas Tree* © Robert Duncan. For more information on this and other images by this artist please visit www.RobertDuncanStudios.com or call 1-800-282-0954

Cover design copyrighted 2006 by Covenant Communications, Inc.

Published by Covenant Communications, Inc.
American Fork, Utah

Copyright © 2006 by Kathryn Jenkins
All rights reserved. No part of this book may be reproduced in any format or in any medium without the written permission of the publisher, Covenant Communications, Inc., P.O. Box 416, American Fork, UT 84003. The views expressed within this work are the sole responsibility of the author and do not necessarily reflect the position of Covenant Communications, Inc., or any other entity.

Printed in the United States of America
First Printing: October 2006

11 10 09 08 07 06   10 9 8 7 6 5 4 3 2 1

ISBN 978-1-59811-207-8

Carolyn was growing increasingly frantic as Christmas approached. It was already the first week in December, and for the first time ever, she had no plan. None at all. It was almost three, and she moved quickly and quietly between her darkened bedroom and the large living room window—keeping vigil over her sleeping husband one minute, watching for the school bus to rumble up to the corner the next.

She wrapped her sweater more tightly against a sudden chill and looked toward the corner again. A slight wind scattered the dry brown leaves across the lawn, and the bare branches of the spindly maple tree in the front yard seemed to scratch the dull gray sky. The bus would be here any minute. She needed to plug in the Christmas tree lights for the children—needed to send their twinkling cheer into the winter afternoon.

Suddenly they burst noisily through the front door, chased by a blast of cold that matched Carolyn's mood. Mark scampered around the corner and down the hall to his bedroom. Katy moved much more slowly, almost cautiously. Carolyn brushed a kiss against her forehead.

"How was school today, honey?"

"I don't know," Katy responded with a shrug of the shoulders. She stood motionless, seemingly mesmerized by the multicolored lights that caused the strands of tinsel to sparkle against the fragrant evergreen branches. She focused on the handful of gifts scattered under the tree, lost in the thoughts that had haunted her for several months.

Aware of Carolyn's hand on her arm, Katy clutched her book bag more firmly and started to move toward the kitchen. She didn't want to talk about it—especially not to her mother.

"A penny for your thoughts," Carolyn whispered, using one of their favorite games in an attempt to identify the sorrow swirling through Katy's mind. She fell into step and moved with her daughter to the counter where the plump green cookie jar sat filled with oatmeal raisin cookies. Katy dropped her book bag on the floor, lifted the lid off the cookie jar, fingered a cookie, then put it back.

"Come on, Katy," Carolyn coaxed. "Why won't you tell me what you want for Christmas?" Carolyn thought of the stash of gifts for Mark, tucked away in the locked cedar closet against the far wall of the garage. There were a few small items there for Katy, but nothing more. She had refused to give the slightest hint about what she wanted, and Carolyn was completely lost.

"'Cause," Katy said quietly.

"Because . . . why?" Carolyn asked, the words threatening to catch in her throat. "Katy, is it because Daddy is so sick?"

"No." The silence fell over them like a smothering blanket; somewhere in the background, Carolyn was aware of Mark dumping a pile of Lincoln Logs onto the floor in his room. Somewhere in the same background, out of the perimeter of the suffocating silence between her and Katy, she heard Glen's ragged cough. He was awake.

"Then what, honey? You need to tell me, so Daddy and I can buy you the present you really want." Carolyn tried hard to remain calm, to shove the swelling panic back beneath the surface.

"I thought *Santa Claus* brings that present," Katy said with an uncharacteristically edgy tone.

"Of course, Katy," Carolyn said, "he *does*." A smile crept across Carolyn's face. It had been their secret for nine years now: it was their *tradition*. Glen always tucked in one very special gift each year, right among the things Santa brought. Neither Katy nor Mark had ever known that the most special gift each year was from their daddy.

"Then I'll tell *Santa* what I want. If he's the one who brings the present, he's the only one who needs to know."

Of course Santa *could* bring the gift . . . but Carolyn knew how important their tradition was to Glen—and that this would be his last opportunity to creep into the living room and place his special offering among the gifts left for his children. She forced a nonchalant expression to match the pretended unassuming pitch in her voice. "But Daddy and I need to know, so we can get you something that goes along with whatever you want the very most."

Katy narrowed her eyes ever so slightly and stared at Carolyn. "Mom, we're going to see Santa in Salt Lake on Saturday, right?" Carolyn nodded. "Okay. I'll tell him then. Or maybe Mrs. Claus. But I'm not telling anyone else. Then . . ." her voice trailed off, small and uncertain.

"Then . . . what?" Carolyn almost dreaded the answer.

"Then, if Santa is not the one who really brings the present, I'll know for sure. Because the present won't be here." Katy scooped up her book bag and went to her room, closing the door behind her. Carolyn felt hot tears sting her eyes as she went to check on Glen.

Playing with his trucks, Mark made the guttural sounds of an eighteen-wheeler in the next room as Carolyn slid cautiously into bed beside Glen. Since the cancer had metastasized to his liver, even gentle movement tended to cause gut-wrenching pain. Glen didn't complain, but Carolyn had seen him wince too often not to make the association.

Weakened from the latest round of chemotherapy, it was an effort for Glen to turn and face Carolyn. Situated against a cluster of feather pillows, he smiled as he tried to drape his arm across her. "Hi, how are the kids?"

Sheltered in the dusk of the bedroom, the heavy drapes drawn between her and the afternoon light that filtered across the valley, Carolyn began to cry. "Oh, Glen, Katy's wondering if there's really a Santa Claus." A small hiccup caught in her throat.

Glen sunk back against the pillows. It had been inevitable . . . the stress of his illness, going on four years now, had finally taken its toll on his blue-eyed nine-year-old. She was too young to make sense out of this—to figure out why he had left her for half an hour at the daddy-daughter dance while he threw up at the edge of the meetinghouse parking lot, where no one could hear him retching. He had fought so hard—had faced his demons down with all the ferocious might he could muster—but still he had created a world that his two innocent children could no longer trust. The frayed edges of all that his cancer represented now threatened to rob his little girl of a belief that had delighted and amazed her since she had first nestled into Santa's lap at the age of two.

"Sweetheart, don't worry. It'll be okay. She'll figure it out."

"It's not that," Carolyn said. "She won't tell me what she wants for Christmas. She's conducting a test, Glen: she's going to tell Santa what she wants, but no one else. Then if the gift isn't here on Christmas morning . . . Of course the gift will be here. But I had hoped . . . had wanted you to be able to give the most special gift, just one more time."

Tears slid unchecked down Glen's cheeks. He and Carolyn had started working even before autumn turned the evenings crisp to make sure that this Christmas would be wonderful. They both knew it would be his last—and they were both determined to make it a holiday that their two children would forever cherish.

They wept silently, side by side, lost in the memories of decades earlier. Glen remembered being just a year older than Katy, still paralyzed by sadness after his mother's death just months earlier. She had gone into town in the quiet little corner of Michigan where they lived and had been struck and killed by a streetcar while her three dark-eyed children waited at home for her to return. That Christmas there had been no tree, no lights, no stockings hung by the hearth. Those had been their mother's jobs, and their grief-stricken father had completely surrendered the holiday in his wild desperation. Glen remembered huddling with his two sisters—one older, one younger—as they wept not only for their mother, but also for the death of Christmas. He had promised himself on that frosty Michigan morning that he would never fail his own children in that way. That he would make Christmas very special, no matter what it took.

Now there was Katy.

Carolyn made one last round in the bedroom to make sure Glen was comfortable. She and the children would be gone all day, meandering along State Street to the bustle of Salt Lake City. She had arranged with their home teacher to check in on him several times during the day but still felt uneasy leaving him that long. As she pulled the patchwork quilt up around his now-thin shoulders, he took her hand in his.

"It's going to work," he said, a smile teasing the corners of his mouth. "I know it will, sweetheart. It's the perfect solution."

"I hope so." She bent and kissed his forehead.

"It will. If I know anything about you, it's how amazingly you're able to send your prayers heavenward and get them right to the front of the line," he teased. "Who knows? You could have moved to top priority ahead of President Kennedy's latest crisis in Cuba, or an impending war, or even a crumbling regime."

She chuckled as she tenderly stroked his cheek. He looked so wan and gray against the pillows. With every passing day, she saw a little more of him slip away; with every passing day, she saw a little more of the life seep out of his eyes. She knew he summoned every fiber of his energy to hide that awful reality from her, but she saw it nonetheless. The fact that he worried so about his little girl in the face of his own demise made her love him all the more.

"Well, you'd better say a prayer for us, too!" she smiled. "Maybe we'll just have to wear Him out with our requests."

He laughed softly. "Carolyn, He loves Katy even more than we do. He'll make sure our last Christmas together is just as it should be."

She was sure of that, too. But what if His idea of the perfect holiday *wasn't* the ability for her to find that one perfect gift—the one Katy most wanted—so that Glen could secretly give it to Katy? What if that wasn't to be part of this last Christmas with her daddy? Carolyn fought against the tendency to crash effortlessly back into despair. She needed to trust more in Him.

She slipped her hand into the pocket of her tweed car coat and clutched the folded paper, just to make sure it was still there. Maybe Glen was right. Maybe this *would* work.

The kids clamored onto the escalator at Auerbach's Department Store in downtown Salt Lake City. Carolyn knew that Santa also visited the J.C. Penney store on

Center Street in downtown Provo, much closer to their home in Orem. But this was tradition. She had chosen this particular visit for her children years ago, and for good reason. When he visited Auerbach's, Santa brought Mrs. Claus along. She had round, rosy cheeks and the kindest eyes Carolyn had ever seen, circled by wire-rimmed glasses. She wore her white hair in a bun at the nape of her neck, reminding Carolyn of her own mother.

But that wasn't all. There on the third floor, at the top of the escalators, was always a makeshift enclosure scattered with straw. And there, nudging the edge of the enclosure, was Rosy Doe—one of Santa's real-live reindeer. Carolyn loved the wide-eyed wonder in the eyes of her children as they gingerly approached Rosy Doe, as they cautiously reached out to pet her soft nose. She delighted in their excitement as they read Christmas books—loved the way they pointed at pictures of Santa and his reindeer, exclaiming, "There she is! Look, Mama, it's Rosy Doe!" *I would make a trip of a million miles to see that reaction,* she thought as they climbed onto the escalator on the second floor.

And then she saw them. There they were, at the top of the escalators on the third floor, just as they had been all the years before: Santa and Mrs. Claus, sitting together near a cluster of Christmas trees—and Rosy Doe, curled in a nap on the soft straw. Mark squeezed Carolyn's hand tightly; at six, he couldn't wait to talk to Santa. He had enthused for weeks about what he would ask for, and had chattered animatedly all the way to Salt Lake about the reindeer.

Katy fell slightly behind Mark and Carolyn, studying Santa carefully. She couldn't deny it: he looked exactly as he had last year, and the year before that. His suit was just as red, and Mrs. Claus's apron was still just as white and ruffled along the edges. Though Katy talked to him only once a year, Santa's voice seemed alarmingly familiar, almost like that of an old friend. Before she was even consciously aware of it, she recognized his merry laughter.

Katy smoothed the skirt of her red velvet dress and handed her coat to her mother. She wore white tights and black patent leather shoes. Mark had on a suit Glen had bought in Chicago; it had a plaid jacket, and a little plaid bow tie danced against his neck. A photographer was part of the package at Auerbach's, and they always dressed in their best for what had become known as their Christmas portrait.

Katy continued to study Santa as they waited in line for their turn on his lap. Carolyn furtively watched her daughter; her indecisiveness was obvious. Again she clutched at the folded paper in her coat pocket. Again she mentally rehearsed her plan. Again she sent a silent but pleading prayer heavenward, asking for divine help.

At last it was their turn, and Mark broke free from Carolyn's hand to scramble onto Santa's generous lap. The old elf virtually twinkled as he gathered the chubby little boy into his arms and asked if he'd been good.

"Oh, yes!" Mark grinned. "You can ask my mom; she's right over there," he said, pointing to Carolyn. Santa's eyes met Carolyn's, and a knowing smile passed between them. "Once, I hid my sister's doll in the field behind our house because I was really, really mad at her. But then I gave it back and said I was sorry. And I let her sleep with my teddy bear that night." Mark smiled again, trusting that his earnest confession was sufficient in North Pole currency.

Santa laughed deep from his belly—which, Carolyn had to admit, *did* shake like a bowlful of jelly. Mark and Santa chatted amiably for a few minutes, and Mark eagerly related what he most wanted to find on Christmas morning. Carolyn stood quietly, gauging whether she could hear the conversation clearly enough from her vantage point at the edge of Rosy Doe's pen, the roped-off area where they made all the parents wait. As Mark slid off Santa's lap, Mrs. Claus smiled at him and handed him a large peppermint candy cane that she retrieved from a bounteous red bag. Mark then dashed over toward Rosy Doe.

Katy edged slowly toward Santa, obviously lacking her brother's enthusiasm.

"And how are you, young lady?" Santa asked.

Katy perched nervously on his knee, refusing to settle further into his lap. She pulled back slightly, studying his face with great intent. The beard *looked* real. So did the moustache. His wavy white shoulder-length hair was real enough. She had to admit it was the same Santa she had grown to love over the years. He was comfortable, familiar. But she had to make sure.

There was the usual lively banter about being good, and then Santa asked Katy what she wanted for Christmas. Carolyn pressed closer, as close as she could to the velvet ropes that kept the parents in line, hoping to hear at least some of Katy's response.

Katy leaned in as close as she could, so close her lips almost touched Santa's ear. "Santa, this is our secret," she whispered solemnly, so softly the old man could scarcely distinguish her words. "I want a Barbie doll." She leaned back away and abruptly climbed off his knee, struggling to hold back the tears. She didn't know which she wanted more: for the Barbie doll to be there on Christmas morning or for it not to be. She hurried away so quickly that she missed the candy cane Mrs. Claus held out toward her and went to stand next to Mark.

Carolyn inched carefully toward one of the elves outfitted in a green pointed hat. "Please," she said quietly, "I need to get this to Santa." She pressed the folded paper from her coat pocket into the elf's palm.

"Umm . . ." the elf looked down at the folded note. "This is kind of unusual . . ."

Carolyn touched the elf lightly on the arm. "Please," she said quietly, "this will probably determine whether my daughter continues to believe in Santa—and whether my husband will have *his* last Christmas wish."

The elf's eyes widened. She stepped over to Santa, who already had another little boy on his lap. The elf stood next to Santa quietly until the child scrambled over to see Rosy Doe. Carolyn watched as the petite, brown-eyed elf leaned to whisper in Santa's ear, then handed him the note. Carolyn quickly glanced at Katy and Mark; they were still petting Rosy Doe, distracted and oblivious to what Carolyn was doing.

Santa quickly opened the folded note and scanned its message. He motioned to the elf and whispered in her ear before tucking the note under his wide black belt, jostling the sleigh bells that were spaced along it.

The elf approached Carolyn quickly. "Your daughter is the one in the red velvet dress?" she whispered.

Carolyn nodded. "She wants a Barbie doll," the elf stated matter-of-factly. "It was the only thing she mentioned."

Relief washed over Carolyn as she smiled her thanks and pressed through the other waiting parents to her children. Glen would be able to deliver the one most special present after all! "Come on, kids," she said, feeling as lighthearted and happy as she had dared to feel in months. "Let's go get some lunch!"

A light storm had dusted the valley with snow, but as Carolyn eased the big green and white Chrysler into the garage, she noticed the driveway and sidewalks had been shoveled. *The home teacher,* she thought, mentally adding this kindness to the long list of ways in which he had served their family during the last several years.

She was surprised and happy to see Glen sitting at the kitchen table.

"Warren just left," he told her. "We had a great talk. It's sure nice to be able to visit." A smile swept across his face, but Carolyn could easily see the sadness in his eyes. She knew how he missed going to work every day at the steel plant—clutching his metal lunchbox in his hand, hollering greetings to the groups of men he supervised in the open hearth. They had become much more than employees; they were friends, and she knew he missed their good-natured banter. While the cancer had been confined to his colon, he had managed to keep working—missing time for several surgeries, staying home during the roughest parts of the chemo.

But once the cancer had invaded his liver, he became too weak to continue working, and the pain medication made it unsafe for him to operate the machinery that forged the steel.

She knew, too, that Glen missed chatting over the chain-link fence with the neighbors next door as they all mowed their lawns—missed the convivial association of friends and neighbors in the everyday business of life. The pain and disease had clearly taken their toll on him, but the loneliness had worked its own unique devastation.

The plaid flannel shirt he wore hung from his frame. When they had met eleven years earlier, he had been robust and muscled; six feet four and nine years older than she, with black hair and eyes so dark they glistened like ebony, Glen had easily swept Carolyn off her feet. He fiercely wanted a family—a desire that stemmed in part from the pieces of him that had been left behind in Michigan. Less than a year after the death of his mother—a dark-haired beauty with a thin face and delicate features—his father had arrived home one afternoon with a woman. She was, as Glen remembered, *round*. It was the best way to describe her. Her makeup was garish, and her tower of hair was an unnatural shade of orange. Her round, full lips were swathed in bright red lipstick, and she teetered on what seemed impossibly high heels. Glen and his two sisters had abruptly stopped a game they were playing under the spreading branches of an oak tree to watch as their father pulled Minnie from the car.

"This is your new mother," he had brusquely announced, pushing Minnie toward them. It was the first time they had seen her.

Glen's life had never been the same. His father had become harsh and abusive; Minnie had been detached—more annoyed by the children than anything. At fourteen, Glen woke up one day and determined to claim his freedom. He hitchhiked to Chicago, where he told the personnel office at U.S. Steel that he was eighteen. Tall and broad-shouldered and mature for his age, there was no reason to doubt it, and Glen started the career that eventually led him to the Geneva Works in Orem. From the moment Minnie had weaved out of the car that afternoon, Glen had vowed that family was more important than anything—and that he would create for his own children the family he so sorely missed as a child.

Katy had come quickly and almost effortlessly, eleven months into his marriage to Carolyn. Mark had followed three years later, after months of disappointment and a myriad of visits to doctors. Close on Mark's heels had come the cancer . . . Glen's two children meant the world to him. They had, quite literally, kept him alive these past few years. More than one of his team of physicians had marveled that he was still alive—in awe of his grit and determination. None of them realized that ever present on the cinema of his mind was his slender, dark-eyed mother, who left to run errands and who never returned—and his own resolve to keep his little family together.

Carolyn bent to circle Glen's now-frail frame in her arms. "It's so good to see you up." She smiled. "Are you hungry?"

"Actually, Warren brought some soup, and we ate together," he explained. "Some of Betty's chicken noodle—so good."

The sounds of the television drifted in from the living room, and Glen knew Katy and Mark were watching a favorite afternoon cartoon show. "So, how did it go?" he asked cautiously. Carolyn's eyes met his with obvious delight. "That good?" he asked.

"That good," she replied. "We're set!" Lowering her voice to a barely discernible whisper, she added, "She wants a Barbie. I'll take care of it on Monday." Carolyn thought again of the locked cedar closet on the far side of the garage and imagined its bounty complete with a treasured Barbie doll.

"Maybe I'll come with you." Glen laughed. "Suddenly I seem to be feeling so much better!"

Glen was too weak to go shopping on Monday. As it turned out, though, only the most intrepid of hale and healthy shoppers could have withstood the demands of shopping for a Barbie doll. Carolyn started at J.C. Penney—the biggest department store in the valley, and certainly the most likely to have a row of Barbie dolls on the shelves in the toy department. But there was not a Barbie in sight. Not a single one of the glamorous figures in their narrow boxes.

Undeterred, Carolyn broadened her search to a handful of other stores along Provo's Center Street. She even scoured the shelves in a family-owned hardware store that smelled of fresh-sawn lumber and that often carried an assortment of toys and games along the back wall. As the day wore on and her optimism wore thin, Carolyn went from one end of the valley to the other in search of the elusive Barbie doll. She had seen ads for the doll in the pages of the *Ladies Home Journal* and *McCall's,* and had watched as the doll had been advertised on television since summer. *Of course,* she thought, feeling a little foolish—*every little girl is going to want one for Christmas. It's going to be a little harder to find one. I guess I'll have to go to Salt Lake.*

The next morning she watched Katy and Mark climb up the steps of the school bus at the corner and waved to them as it lurched away from the curb. As soon as it was out of sight, she dashed to get ready for her clandestine errand. With any luck, she would be able to get there and back before the kids got home from school. After situating Glen in the living room with a good book, she backed the Chrysler down the sloping driveway and started the drive to Salt Lake. Turning the knob on the car radio, she found her favorite station; the Christmas carols that drifted through the air fueled her enthusiasm. The spirit of Christmas—of Santa—filled her heart. To her, it seemed as though she was on the errand of angels.

With Christmas only two weeks away, downtown Salt Lake City was festive, crowded with shoppers who juggled packages and hurried along the sidewalks, ducking in and out of shops. Swags of evergreen garland were draped along the street lights, and wreaths festooned with large red bows decorated the store fronts. Carolyn finally found a parking space near ZCMI and stopped to admire the holiday scenes in the store's tall windows before making her way to the toy department on the third floor.

Carolyn easily found the section where dolls were arranged in neat rows and worked her way past lifelike baby dolls to the more sophisticated dolls—dolls for older girls. Girls like Katy. She eagerly scanned the shelves. Surely, a top seller like the Barbie doll would be displayed prominently, easy to see. She looked two times. Three.

There were no Barbie dolls. *If only I had been able to shop earlier!* Carolyn chided herself. Back out in the freezing December air, Carolyn walked the three blocks to Auerbach's. *It's not as popular as ZCMI,* she reasoned. *Not as many people shop there. Maybe they'll still have some Barbie dolls.*

The shelves in Auerbach's toy department were much more picked over than those in ZCMI had been. Carolyn asked to speak to the manager.

"I need a Barbie doll," she explained with as much urgency as she could muster.

A weary smile spread over the manager's face. "I'm so sorry, ma'am," he responded matter-of-factly. "That's not going to happen. We didn't even *receive* any Barbie dolls this year."

"Your store didn't get any Barbie dolls?"

"No, no, not our *store,*" the manager explained. "Our *area.* There were no Barbie dolls shipped to the state of Utah."

Carolyn's heart plunged, and her stomach formed a tight knot. The manager looked at this mother—so like the other mothers he had seen and talked with this season—and tried to explain the situation.

"Mattel—the company that manufactures Barbie—first introduced her at the New York Toy Show three years ago," he said. "Buyers weren't enthusiastic; she was too different from the typical baby dolls that have been so popular. But the public was another story. Demand has been so great that Mattel is still struggling to catch up with orders. She was shipped to the West Coast and the East Coast and a couple of major cities like Chicago and St. Louis, but they wouldn't even *look* at us in Utah." He hoped it didn't sound too well-rehearsed; he was boggled by the number of times he'd had to explain the situation since the gift-buying season began in earnest several weeks ago.

Then he saw it: this woman was crying. Openly. Unashamed. He'd seen plenty of disappointed shoppers but none who had actually started crying right there in the toy department. His eyes met hers, and he shifted uncomfortably.

"I apologize," Carolyn sniffled, sensing his discomfort. She swiped at the tears with the sleeve of her coat. "It's just that—my daughter couldn't decide if she still believed in Santa, so she decided to tell *only him* what she wanted for Christmas. She figured if he was real, the gift would be there on Christmas morning. It happened right here—here, at Auerbach's. The real dilemma is that my husband . . . he always gives the gift Katy most wants. I managed to find out that she wanted a Barbie . . . and this is his last Christmas with us . . ." Her voice trailed off.

The manager squarely met her gaze. This was more than a run-of-the-mill shopper who was checking off items on a dog-eared Christmas list. This was a woman who was trying to save *Christmas* for a child whose heart was heavy with doubt and for a husband whose holiday would be his last. He didn't know *what,* but there had to be *something* he could do for her.

"I don't know if this will work," he offered, "but I will get you the address and phone number of Mattel's headquarters in Southern California. Maybe they can help . . ." He spun around. "I'll be right back," he called out over his shoulder.

Carolyn stood alone, clutching her black purse and unbuttoning the top of her coat. Her face was hot, and her heart seemed leaden. She almost had to will herself to keep breathing. Other shoppers moved quickly around her, examining the ruffles of doll dresses and grabbing boxes off the shelves. Carolyn's thoughts moved first to Katy, then to Glen—his last Christmas with his little girl. Her thoughts abruptly returned to the toy department as she felt the manager's hand on her arm.

"Here," he said, offering a piece of paper to Carolyn. "I hope this works . . ."

She thought she could detect the despair of dashed dreams in his eyes as he handed her the note. "Thank you so much," she said, taking the address and shoving it into the coat pocket that had cradled her note for Santa only a few days earlier. "You've been very kind."

"Good luck," he said as she started back toward the escalators.

She got home only a few minutes before the school bus was due. Heavy with despair, she sank onto the couch next to Glen and sobbed as she related what she'd learned. There wasn't a Barbie to be had in the state of Utah. She'd come home empty-handed, except for the address and phone number crammed in her coat pocket.

Glen put an arm around her shoulders. "Carolyn, you tried your best," he said through his own tears. "There's nothing more we can do. Let's focus on what we *can* do to make this the best Christmas for everyone in this family."

Nestling her head into his shoulder, Carolyn wept freely—for Katy. For Glen. For lost dreams. For last Christmases. Hearing the unmistakable approach of the school bus, she sat up and wiped her eyes and put a smile on her face for her children.

Six days later, less than a week before Christmas, Carolyn moved in and out of the back door, carrying in groceries for their Christmas Eve dinner. She smiled as she took out the bag of Oreo cookies. Each year, they left Santa a fistful of Oreos on a special saucer, reserved for just that occasion. And each Christmas morning, Santa left them in return a can of black olives that glistened like jewels. It was a sweet tradition that Carolyn cherished, and she tucked the Oreos away in a drawer for Christmas Eve.

Suddenly she looked up to see Glen coming into the kitchen, a warm smile brightening his pain-weary face. "You'll never believe who I just talked to," he teased.

"Who?" Carolyn asked, pushing aside items on a refrigerator shelf to make room for a twelve-pound turkey.

"One of the big shots at Mattel."

Carolyn abruptly stopped what she was doing and turned to study Glen's face.

"I told him about Katy. About Santa. About Barbie. About me. I explained it would be my last Christmas, and that I wanted it to be perfect . . . and that we had tried everything else to make our tradition work." He paused. His eyes filled with tears.

"And?" Carolyn cried.

"And he's going to send me a Barbie doll. One of the blonde ones—the ones that are the most popular. It's one he's kept in his office to show dealers. And, Carolyn . . ." he paused. His smile captured every inch of his face, and his eyes danced. "He's going to send it airmail. If everything works as it should, it will be here on Christmas Eve."

Carolyn fell into his arms, laughing and crying at the same time.

By four-thirty on Christmas Eve, Glen struggled to pull himself off the couch. It was already dusk. The mail had come, and the promised package from Mattel had not been there. Charlie—who had been their mailman for years—had even walked back out to the curb and had looked through his truck again, just to make sure. Glen's heart ached, but there was nothing more they could have possibly done. Carolyn had taken the kids to go pick up her mother in Provo, and they were due back any time. The savory aroma of roasting turkey filled the air, and Glen wanted to change into something a little nicer.

Christmas Eve at their house was as predictable as the sun rising in the morning. They gathered around the table in the kitchen for turkey dinner—complete with creamy mashed potatoes, Carolyn's special stuffing, Waldorf salad studded with walnuts and raisins, cranberry sauce, and hot rolls. Carolyn's mother always brought her signature steamed plum pudding with lemon sauce, a recipe that had made it over the ocean and across the plains from Sweden with *her* mother. Then they gathered in the soft glow of the Christmas tree, and Glen read the story of the Savior's birth from the large, leather-bound family Bible. Then they unwrapped their gifts from each other, one at a time, exclaiming over each one. Throughout the evening, the anticipation for Christmas day built in a steady swell.

This year, that anticipation would be sweet in so many ways, but terrible in others. Glen smiled. Mark still had the uncomplicated expectation of rushing into the living room and finding a stocking stuffed with treats and an array of shiny, new toys spread in front of the couch—offerings from Santa, who had swooped down the chimney sometime during the night. Mark would rush by the saucer, littered with Oreo crumbs, long enough to see the expected can of olives. Then he'd be off, squeals of delight marking each new discovery.

But Katy . . . Katy's anticipation would be something else entirely. And when Glen would not be able to be the one to prop the Barbie up in his red leather chair—where Santa always arranged Katy's stash—what would happen? Glen's own anticipation, he realized, was both sweet and terrible.

As he pulled on a pair of pants and cinched the drawstring waist, the doorbell sliced through the stillness of the house. It was probably the Sorensens from next door—they always brought a plate of home-baked treats on Christmas Eve. This year the exchanges with neighbors had been especially tender; no one expected Glen to survive much past spring. He tried to smile genuinely as he opened the door.

It was Charlie. Their mailman.

"Glen." It was all he could manage to say. He thrust a tattered package wrapped in plain brown paper at Glen. "It just arrived about fifteen minutes ago. I offered to bring it on my way home." The tears began to flow. "Merry Christmas, Glen."

Glen grabbed the box with one hand and wrapped the other arm around the mailman in a warm embrace. "Oh, Charlie, Merry Christmas to you, too." Glen watched through tear-filled eyes as Charlie scurried back down the walk to his car. *Maybe—just maybe—Santa sometimes wears the uniform of the U.S. Postal Service.*

The next morning, just as the sun was starting to peek over the east mountains, Mark's voice split the air. "Come on, everyone!" he cried. "It's Christmas!"

Carolyn helped Glen out of bed and grabbed their robes. It had been a long night. Everything had been done in slow motion . . . done for the last time with Glen.

"Come on, Katy!" Mark yelled. "Hurry!"

It was their tradition. No one could go into the living room until they were all ready.

Katy slowly rounded the corner into the kitchen. Her face was flat, expressionless. Mark was too excited to notice; once his sister appeared, he bolted into the living room. Carolyn and Glen moved slowly toward Katy.

"Come on, honey," Glen said, gesturing. "Let's go see what Santa brought." His eyes sparkled; Carolyn fought back tears.

Katy moved slowly toward the living room door. Mark was already immersed in his stash, running back and forth between Carolyn and his grandmother, eagerly holding up his treasures. Katy looked through the doorway and saw the can of olives sitting on the Christmas Eve saucer. A glimmer of hope raced through her heart.

Finally, she forced herself to move all the way into the living room. Averting her gaze to Mark and his antics, she moved agonizingly in the direction of the red leather chair. Mustering up all the courage she could, she turned and looked.

In one fluid motion she lunged toward the chair and grabbed the Barbie doll.

It was here.

He was real!

Relief and joy washed over her like an avalanche pounding down a mountainside. Holding the Barbie doll in both hands, she sunk to the floor and laughed with the merriment that every child should experience on that morning of all mornings.

Carolyn slipped her hand into Glen's. They stood together on that last Christmas, knowing that it had, indeed, been perfect. The perfect last Christmas.

Four decades later, Katy hung the last of the delicate gold ornaments on the tree and sat back to take in its beauty. It was late—well after midnight—and the only light in the room came from the tiny white lights scattered across the branches of the silk tree. It was a sweet glow, one that carried her mind back across the years to all the Christmases she had known and loved.

The best one—the most bittersweet—was that Christmas of 1962. The year she got the Barbie. The last year she celebrated Christmas with her father.

The story of how the Barbie ended up in the red leather chair had become family lore, a treasured tale that was dusted off and regaled in the best of times. In the decades since then, Katy had worked her own share of miracles around the Christmas celebrations of her own children—though none ever quite measured up to the story of the Barbie doll.

Katy chuckled. How many had been involved in that miracle? Surely Santa, who sat with Mrs. Claus and who tucked the note behind his black leather belt. Certainly the toy manager at Auerbach's, who was moved by a mother's tender tears. Obviously the executive at Mattel, who heard in a father's desperate plea all the hopes and dreams of Christmas. And, without doubt, Charlie—the mailman who never gave up looking for the airmailed package. But most of all, there had been Katy's father. It had been nothing more than a little plastic-molded doll dressed in a sleek swimsuit and packaged in a narrow box—but to her, and to him, it represented the love of a father for his child.

Snuggling into the corner of the couch, illuminated by the glow of Christmas lights, Katy smiled. It hadn't been about Santa at all. It hadn't even been about Barbie. Or about Christmas. It had been about a father's greatest gift for a much-loved daughter. And now, decades later, that's what it was still all about: Jesus of Bethlehem, the Babe wrapped in swaddling clothes—a Father's greatest gift for a much-loved world.

With professional experience in corporate and internal communications, public relations, media relations, marketing communications, and publications management, Kathryn B. Jenkins currently serves as the managing editor at Covenant Communications. Before that, she was press secretary for a U.S. Congressman; vice-president of a Salt Lake City publishing company; manager of strategic communications for a software manufacturer; director of public relations at a private college; and held communications management positions at a variety of national and international corporations. Kathryn is the author or co-author of more than seventy books and wrote an award-winning book-length poetry manuscript. The mother of five and grandmother of one, she lives in American Fork, Utah, where she loves scrapbooking and researching family history.